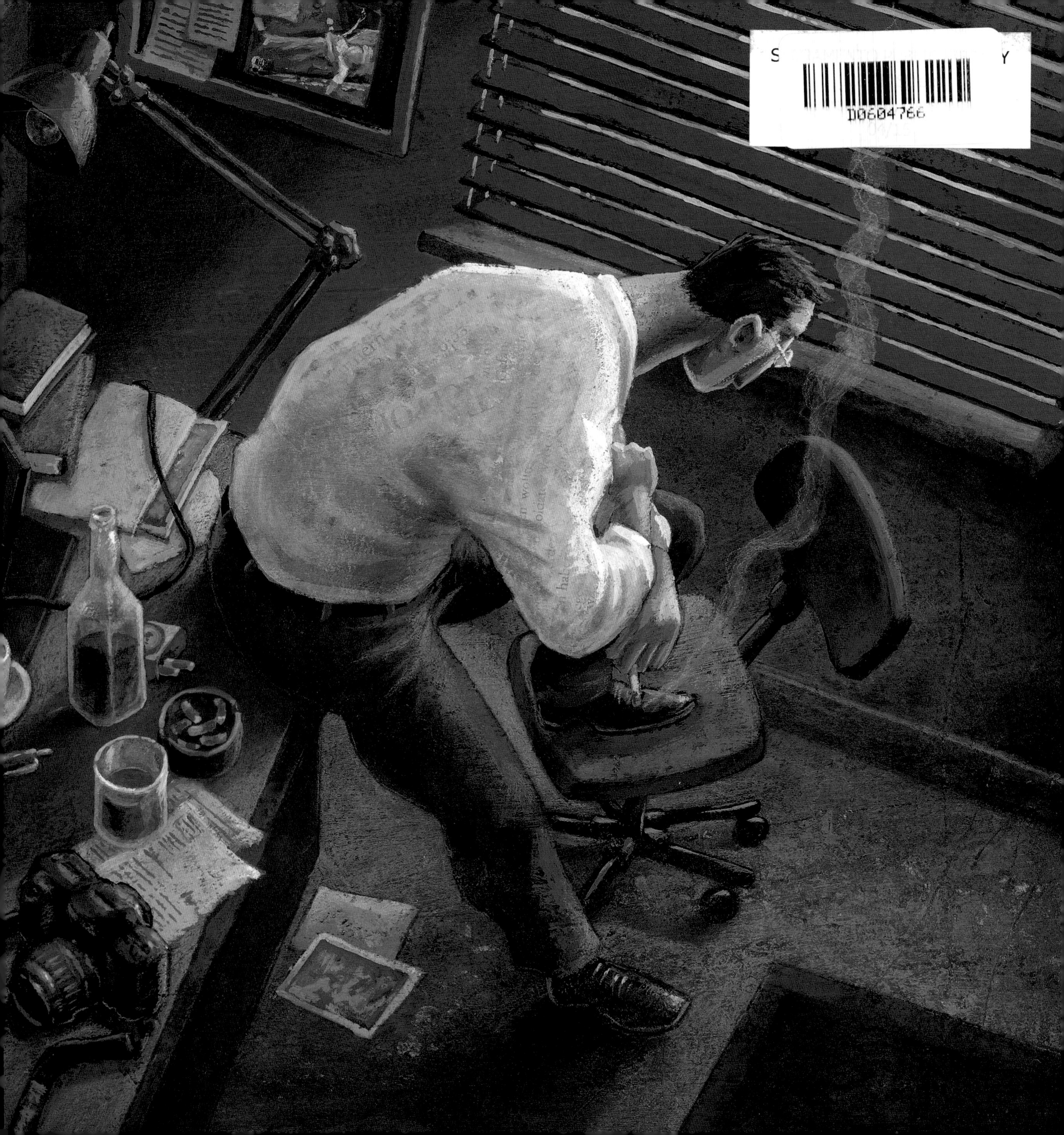

For Kolja, Anika and Tobias.

K.G.

Karin Gruss, born in Wuppertal, was a German teacher and bookseller and oversaw the picture book program at publishing house Peter Hammer Verlag. She currently works as a consultant and instructor on children's and young adult literature in Düsseldorf. *One Red Shoe* is her first picture book, based on impressions of the ongoing conflict in the Gaza Strip.

Tobias Krejtschi, born in 1980 in Dresden, studied illustration at HAW Hamburg and is now a lecturer there. His first picture book, *Crafty Mama Sambona*, with text by Hermann Schulz, received several awards (nominated for the German Children's Literature Award, Troisdorfer Picture Book Prize) and has been translated into multiple languages. *One Red Shoe* was named one of the five Most Beautiful German Books of 2013 in the children's book category by the German Book Art Foundation.

Boje Verlag in the Bastei Lübbe AG

First published in English in 2014 by Wilkins Farago Pty Ltd (ABN 14 081 592 770)
PO Box 78, Albert Park, Victoria 3206, Australia
Teachers' Notes & other material: www.wilkinsfarago.com.au

Printed in China by Everbest Printing Co Ltd

ISBN 978-0-9871099-6-5

Karin Gruss | Tobias Krejtschi

ONE RED SHOE

wf
WILKINSfarago

Luckily I had put my mobile in my back pocket. The explosions and gunshots outside were so loud that I only detected the call because the phone vibrated.

"A school bus has been attacked!" my colleague shouted over the sounds of combat. "The surviving children have just been evacuated."

Strange, how ordinary this message sounded.

"Meet you at the clinic! And keep your head down if you hear gunfire, my friend, we'll need you here!" With that, he hung up.

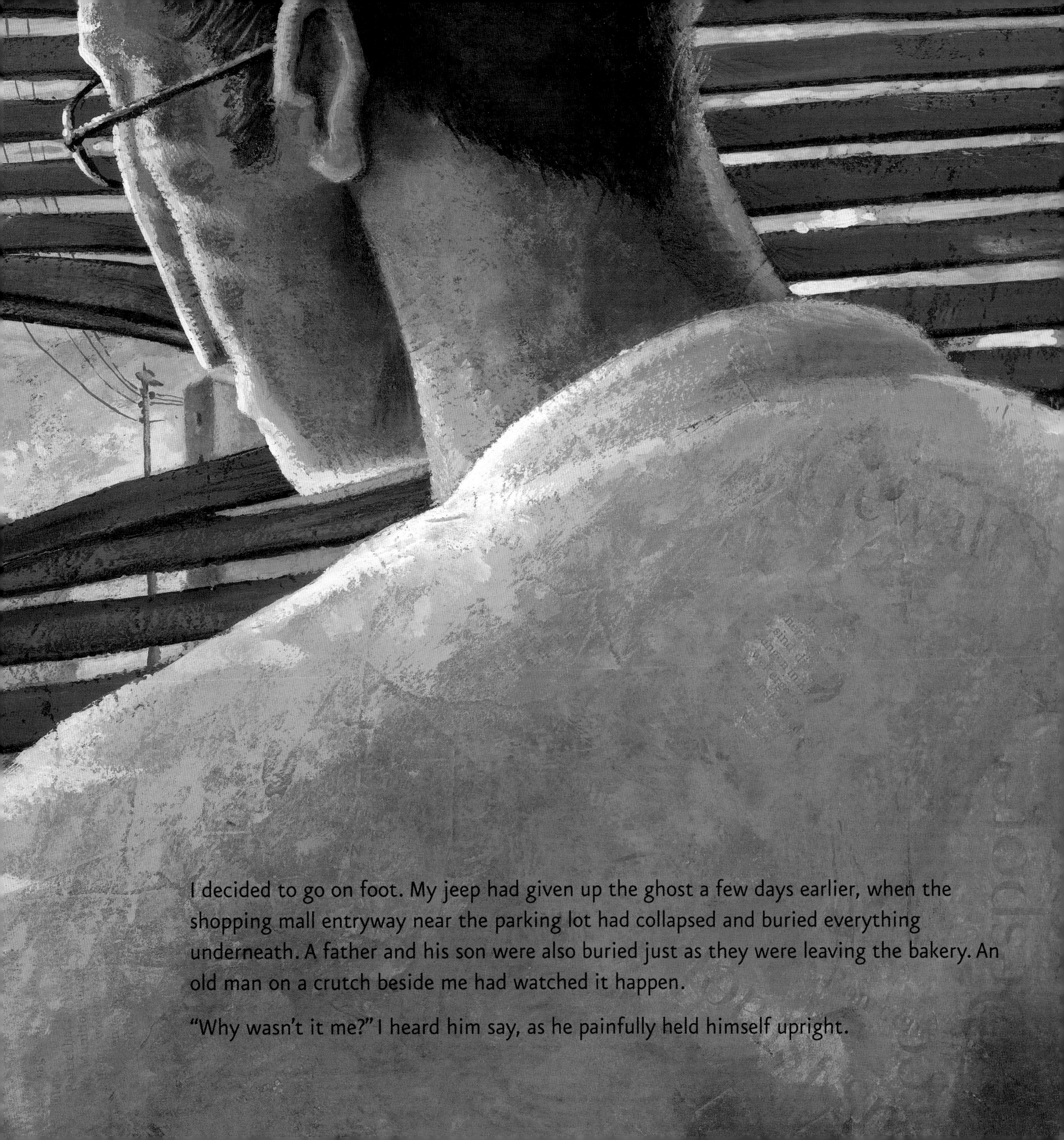

I decided to go on foot. My jeep had given up the ghost a few days earlier, when the shopping mall entryway near the parking lot had collapsed and buried everything underneath. A father and his son were also buried just as they were leaving the bakery. An old man on a crutch beside me had watched it happen.

"Why wasn't it me?" I heard him say, as he painfully held himself upright.

Television crews gathered out in front of the hotel; they had also heard about the attack on the school bus. I hurried along, staying close to the walls of the houses, past playing children.

I held my camera in my hand. You had to be ready for anything.

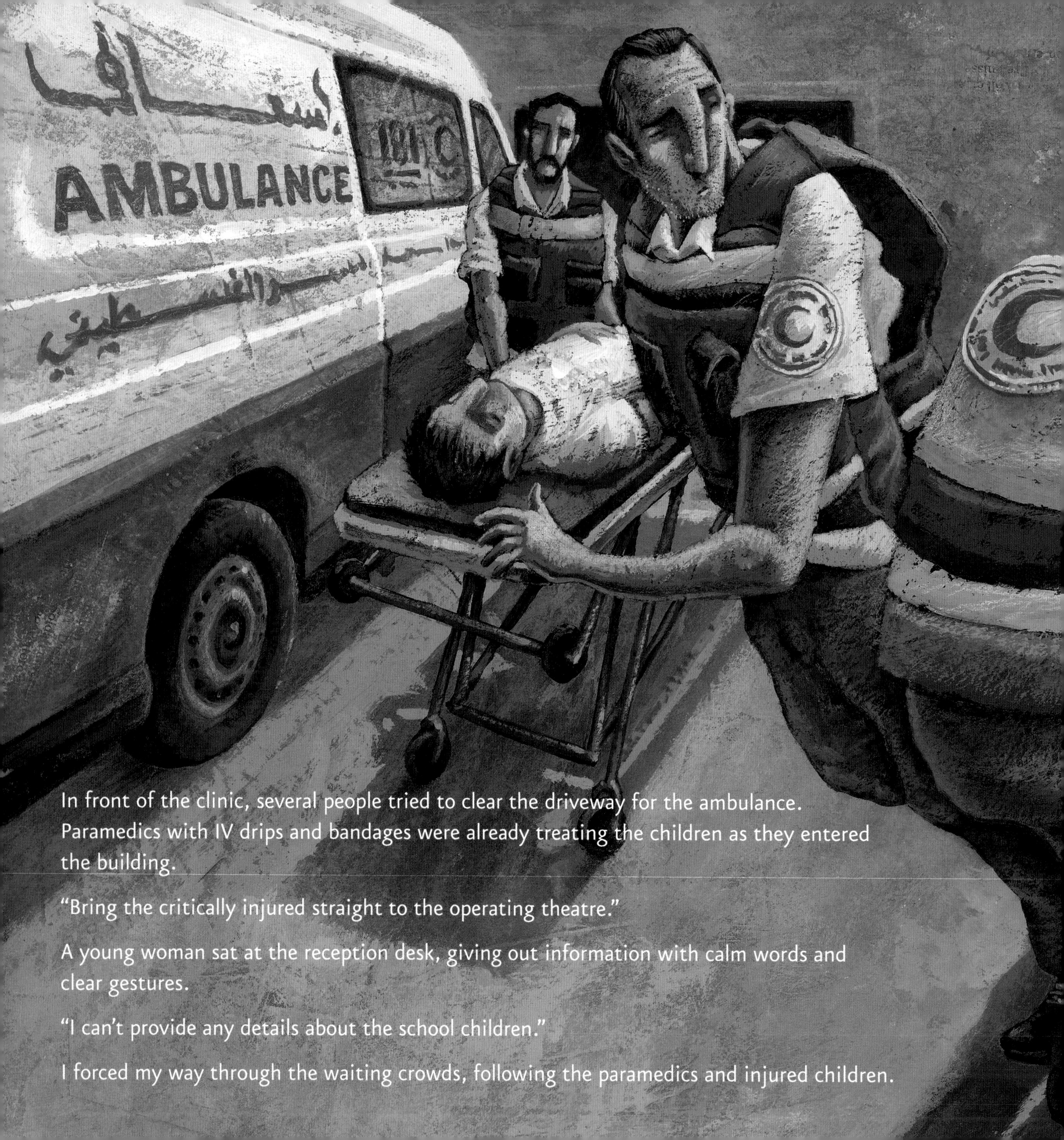

In front of the clinic, several people tried to clear the driveway for the ambulance. Paramedics with IV drips and bandages were already treating the children as they entered the building.

"Bring the critically injured straight to the operating theatre."

A young woman sat at the reception desk, giving out information with calm words and clear gestures.

"I can't provide any details about the school children."

I forced my way through the waiting crowds, following the paramedics and injured children.

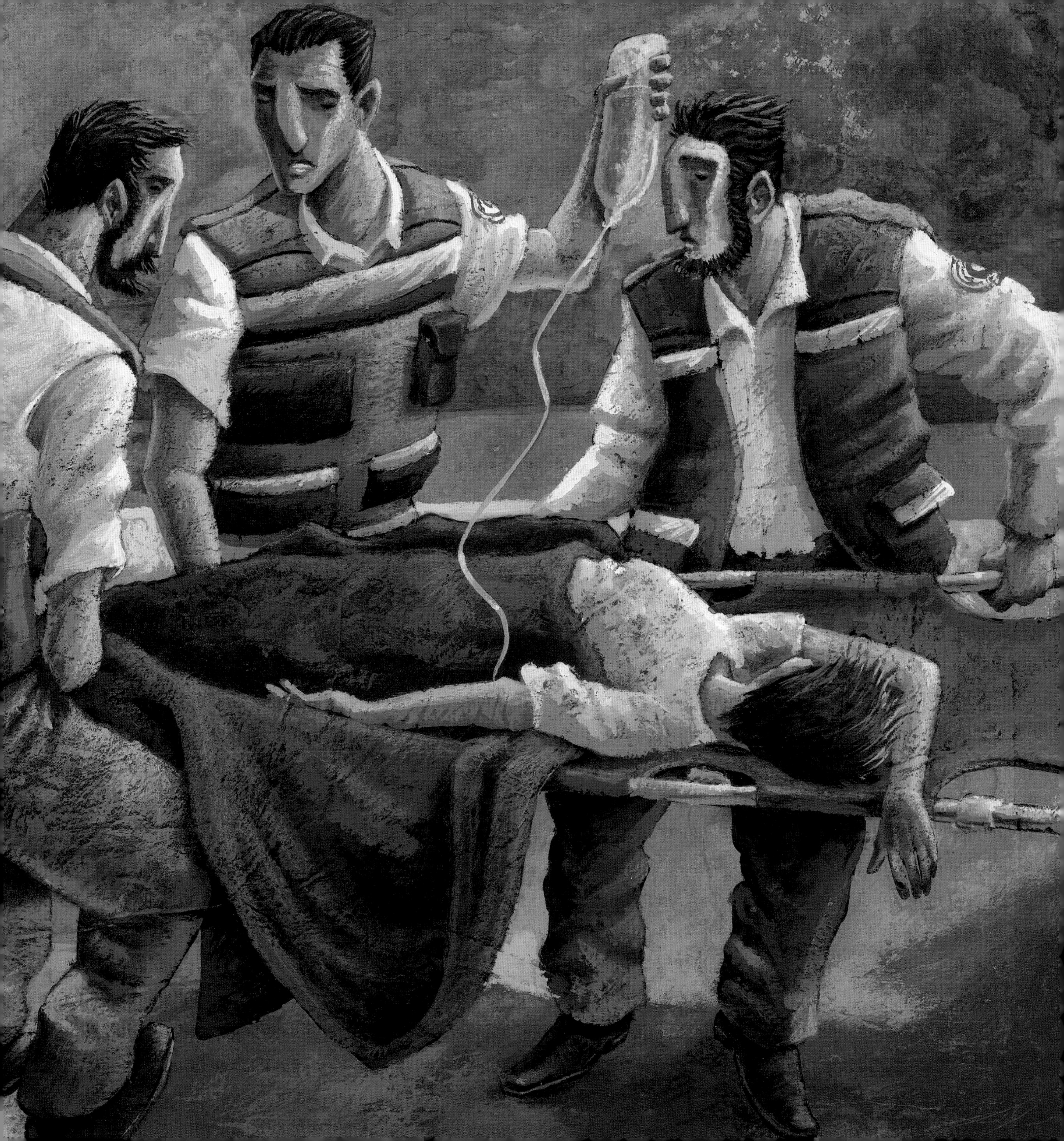

My colleague stood outside the operating theatre.

"He's eight or nine years old," he said. "A grenade hit his right leg. He also has a shrapnel wound to the head."

He pointed to a boy in jeans and a t-shirt who lay on a gurney in front of me. He wore a red basketball shoe on his left foot. I had given a pair of the same shoes to my nephew for his eighth birthday. I turned my camera on.

The red shoe showed up clearly in the foreground of the display. Where had the other one gone? My nephew loved his basketball shoes. It was unimaginable to think he would lose one! Had this boy loved his shoes that much too?

I took another picture from a different angle. After all, this was about the boy, not the shoes! Now the bandage on his head came into focus.

For the first time, I looked at his face. His eyes were closed but his lips moved. It seemed like he was saying his name. Maybe children in wartime learned early on to repeat their names even if they lost consciousness, so that relatives could find them.

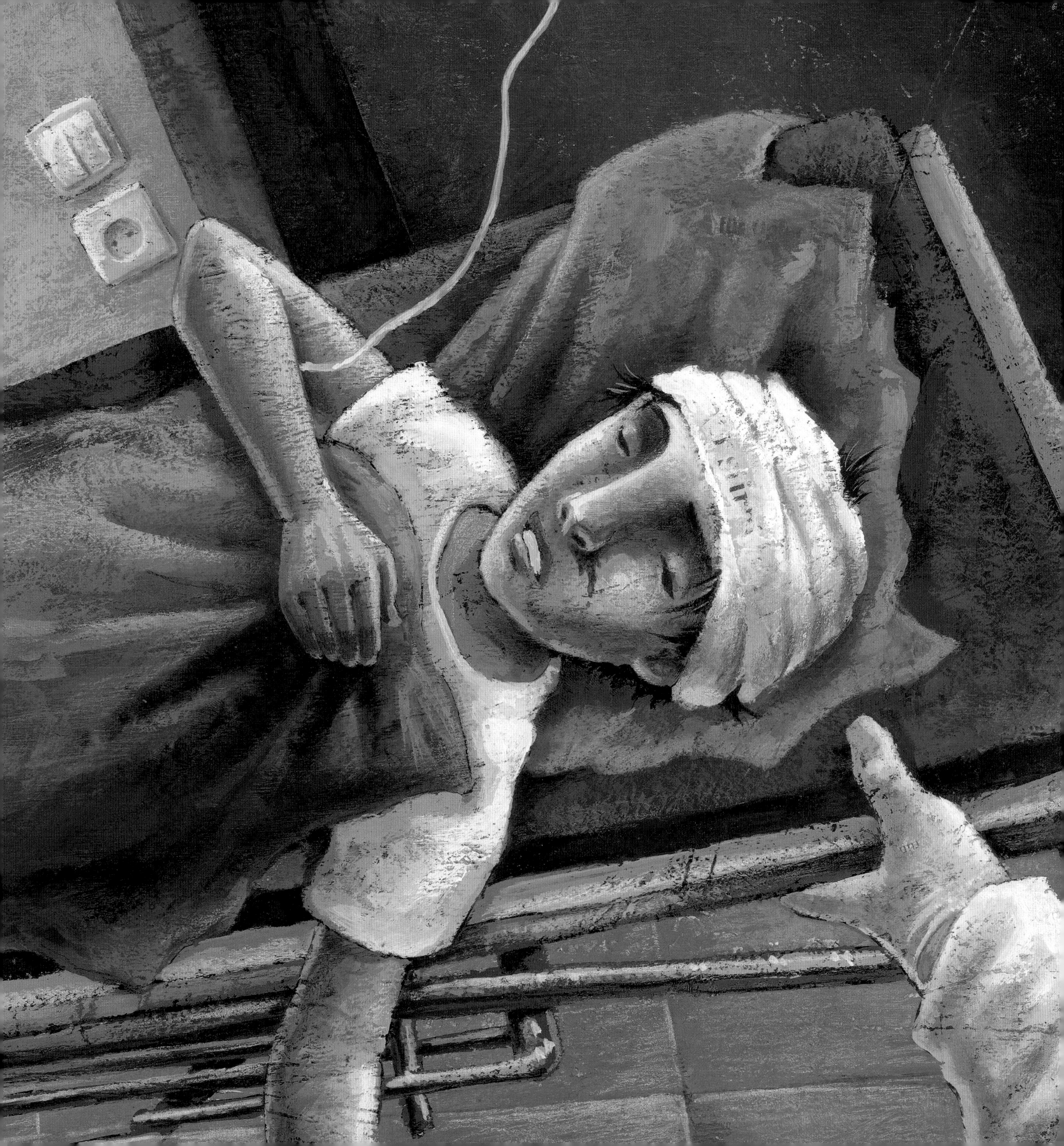

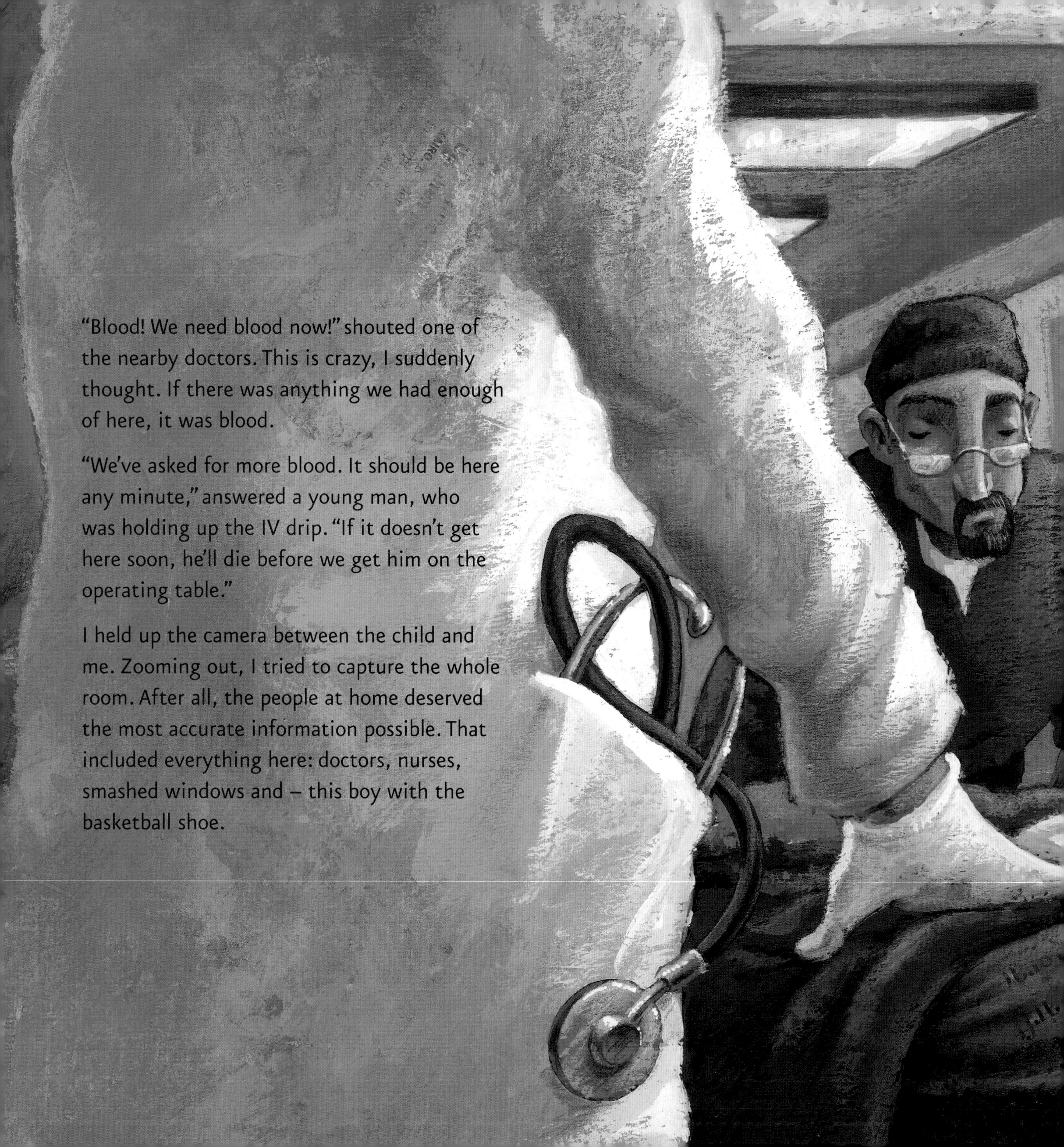

"Blood! We need blood now!" shouted one of the nearby doctors. This is crazy, I suddenly thought. If there was anything we had enough of here, it was blood.

"We've asked for more blood. It should be here any minute," answered a young man, who was holding up the IV drip. "If it doesn't get here soon, he'll die before we get him on the operating table."

I held up the camera between the child and me. Zooming out, I tried to capture the whole room. After all, the people at home deserved the most accurate information possible. That included everything here: doctors, nurses, smashed windows and – this boy with the basketball shoe.

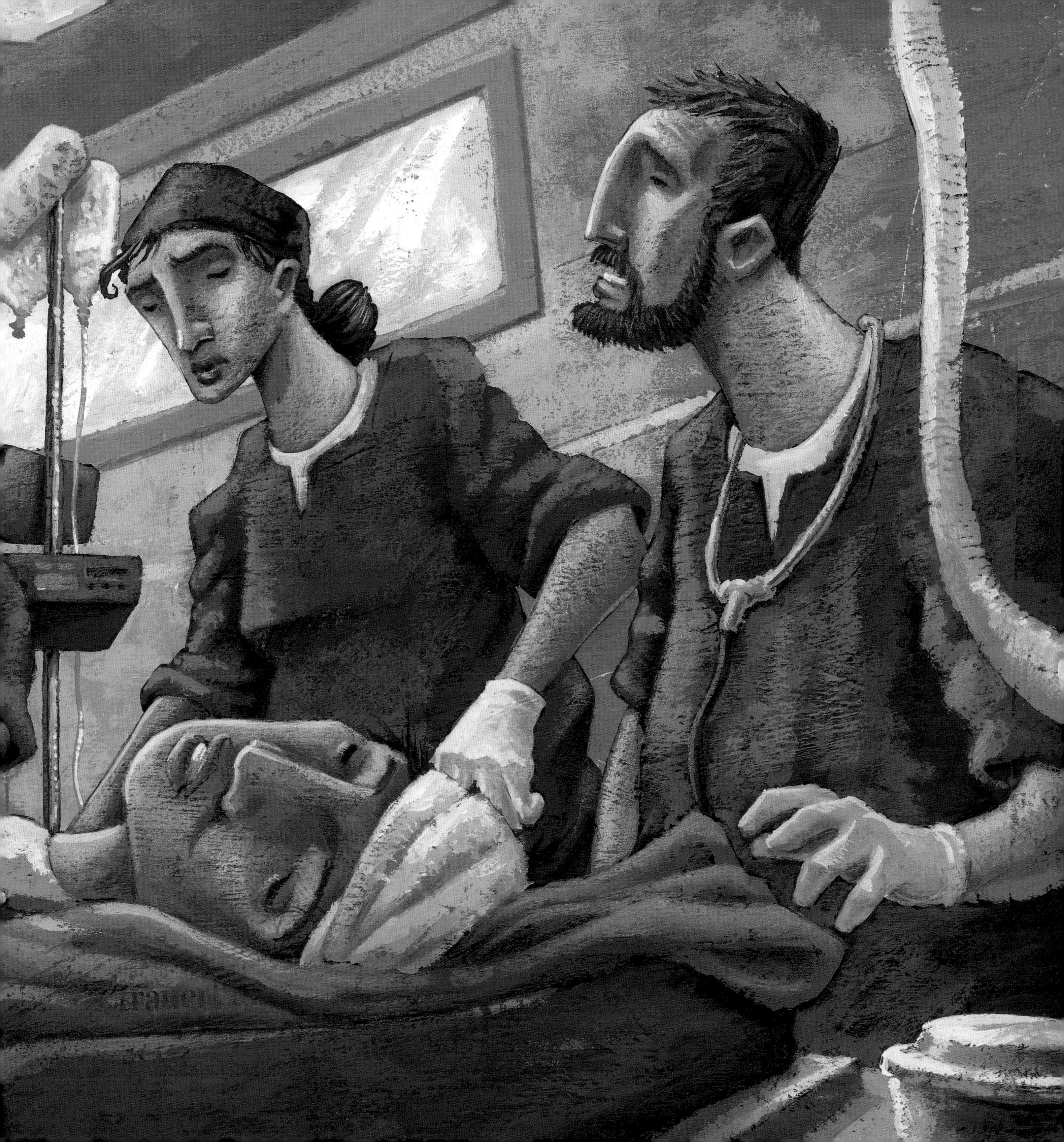

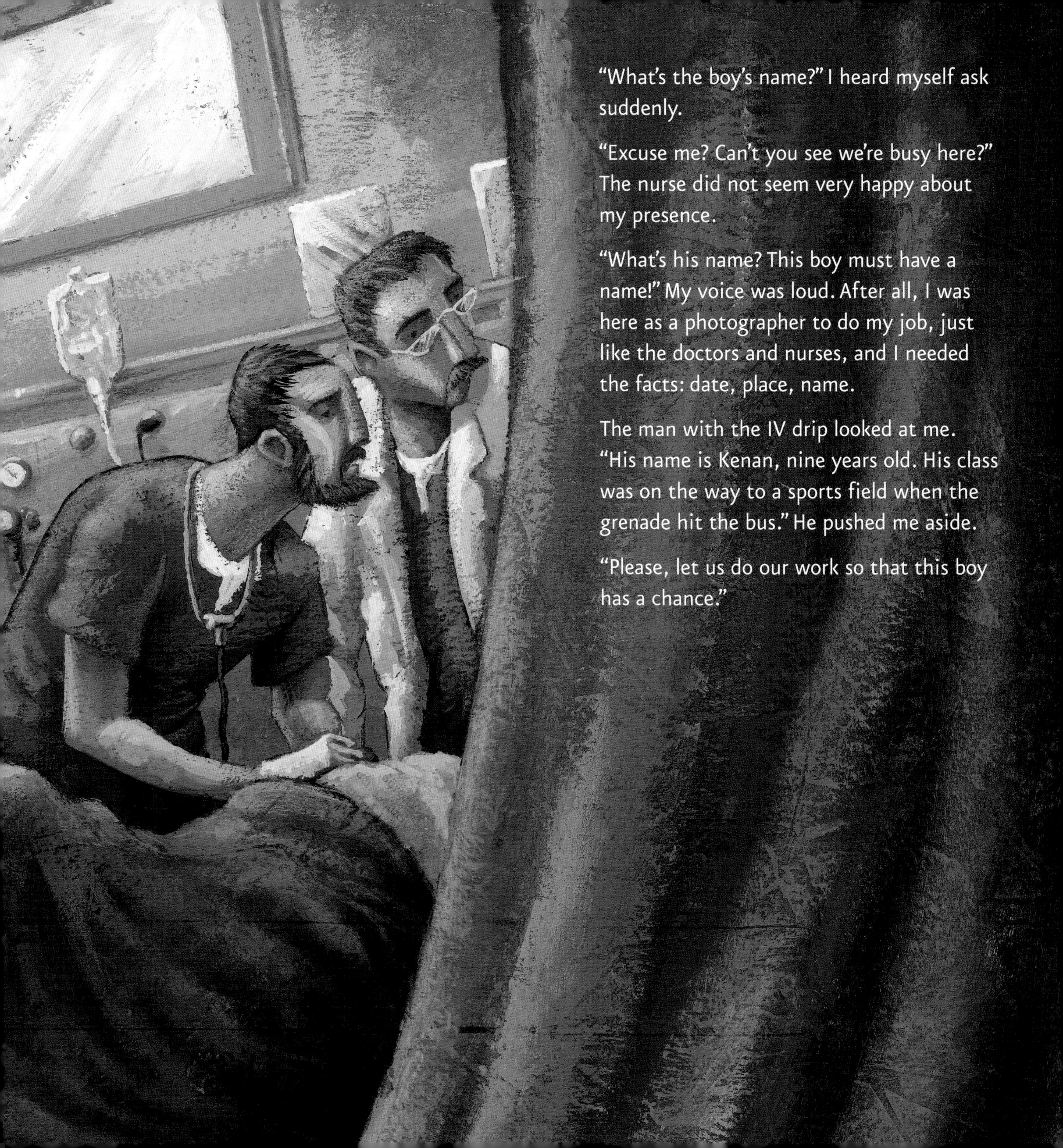

"What's the boy's name?" I heard myself ask suddenly.

"Excuse me? Can't you see we're busy here?" The nurse did not seem very happy about my presence.

"What's his name? This boy must have a name!" My voice was loud. After all, I was here as a photographer to do my job, just like the doctors and nurses, and I needed the facts: date, place, name.

The man with the IV drip looked at me. "His name is Kenan, nine years old. His class was on the way to a sports field when the grenade hit the bus." He pushed me aside.

"Please, let us do our work so that this boy has a chance."

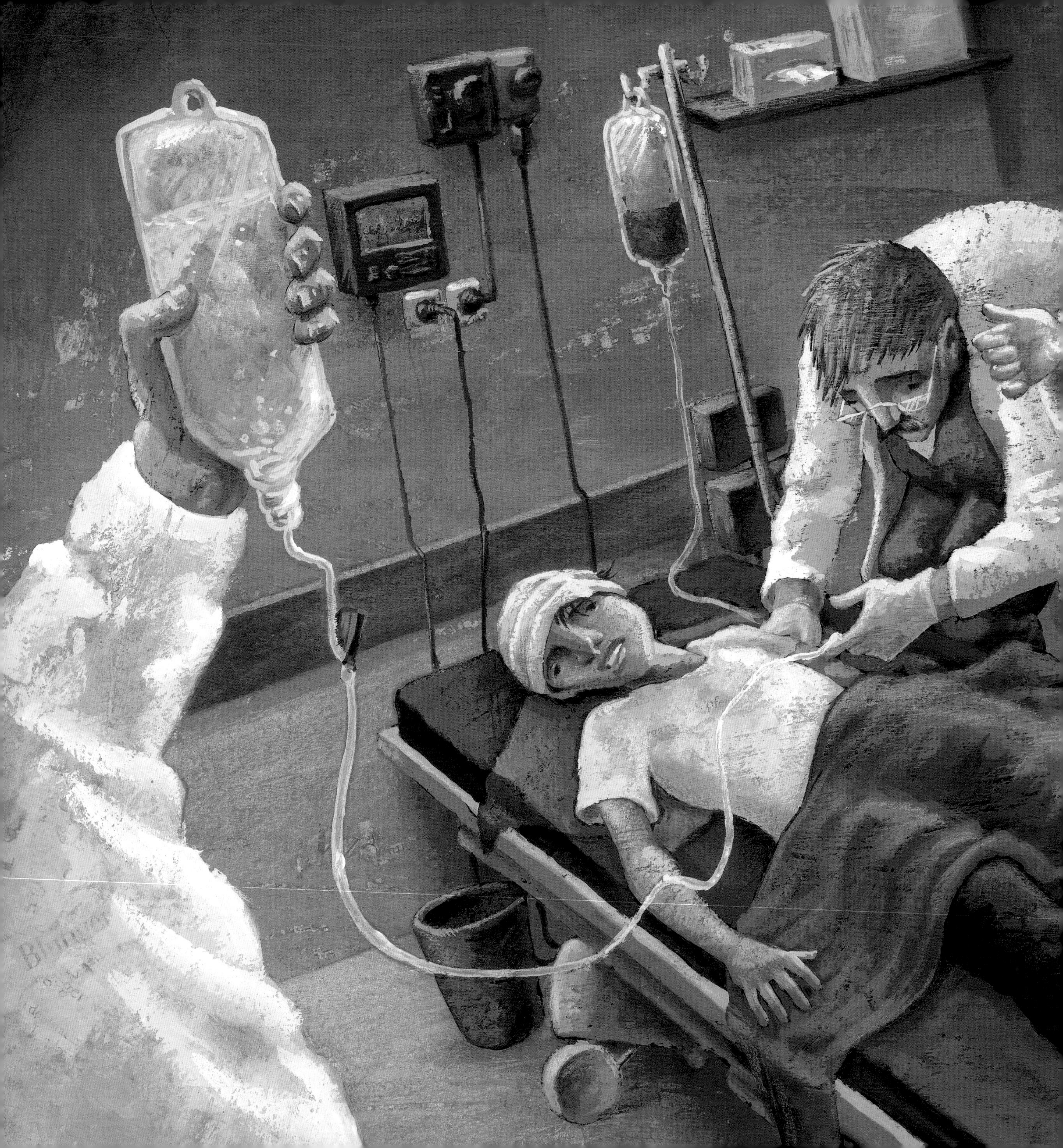

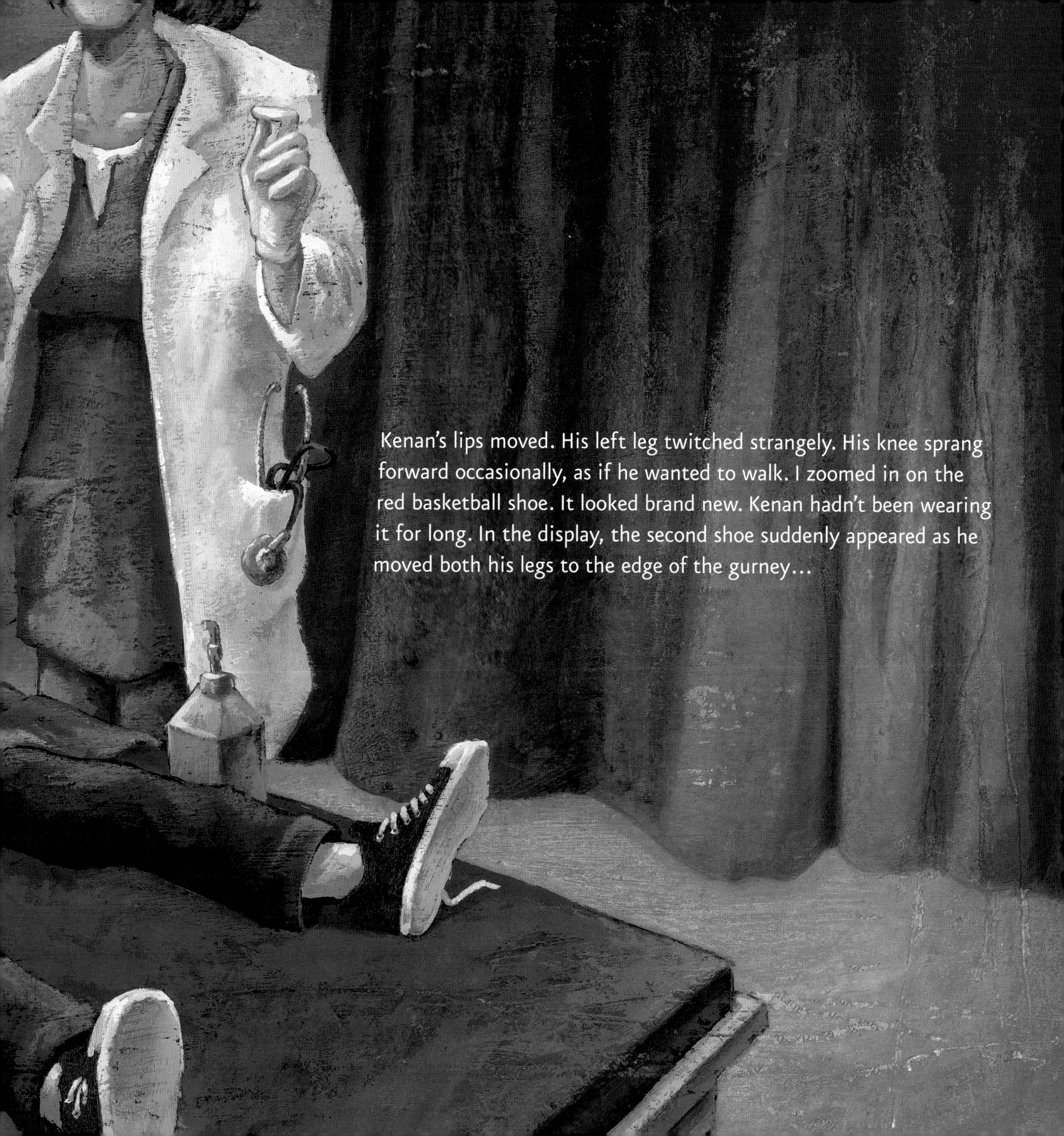

Kenan's lips moved. His left leg twitched strangely. His knee sprang forward occasionally, as if he wanted to walk. I zoomed in on the red basketball shoe. It looked brand new. Kenan hadn't been wearing it for long. In the display, the second shoe suddenly appeared as he moved both his legs to the edge of the gurney…

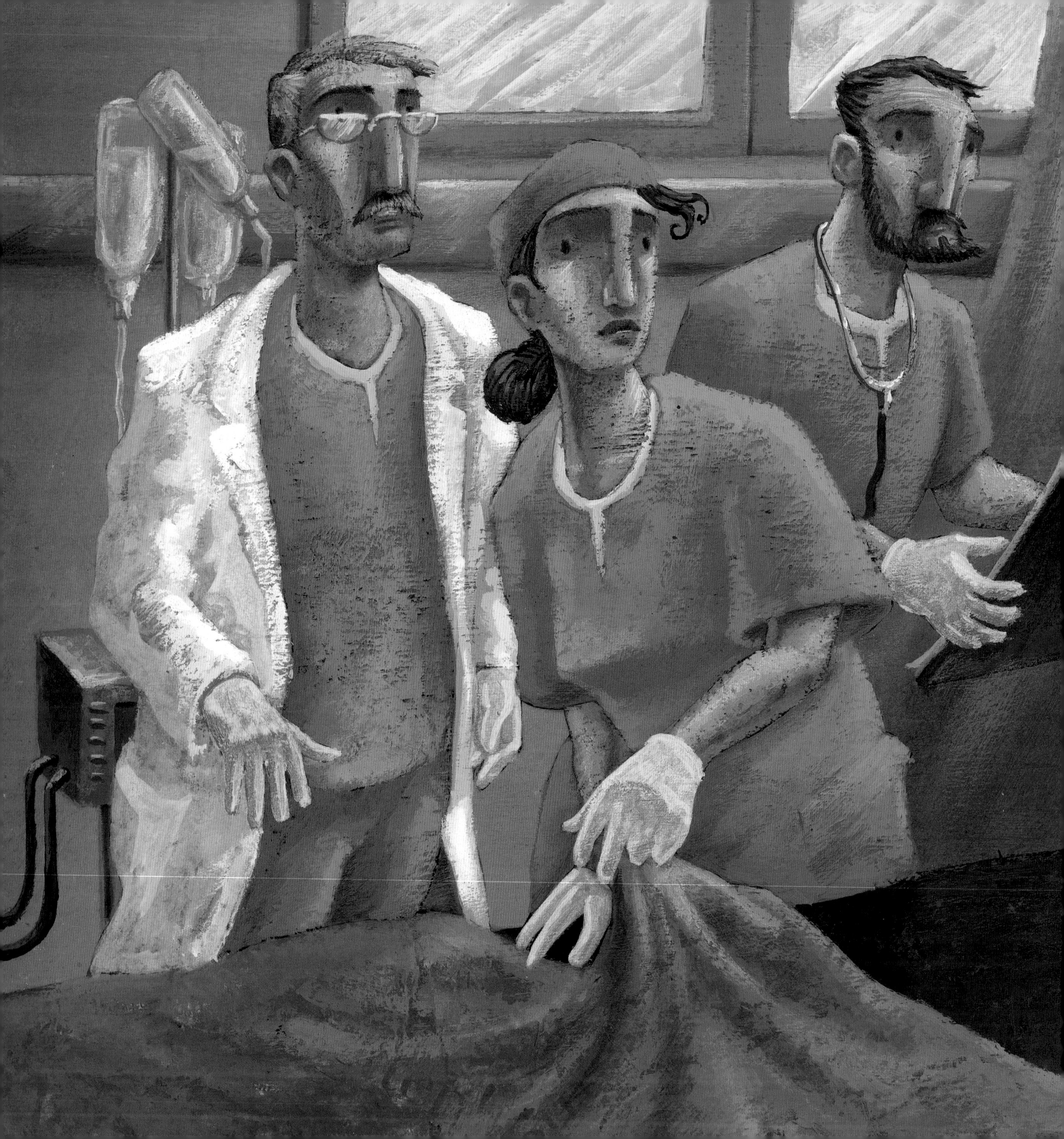

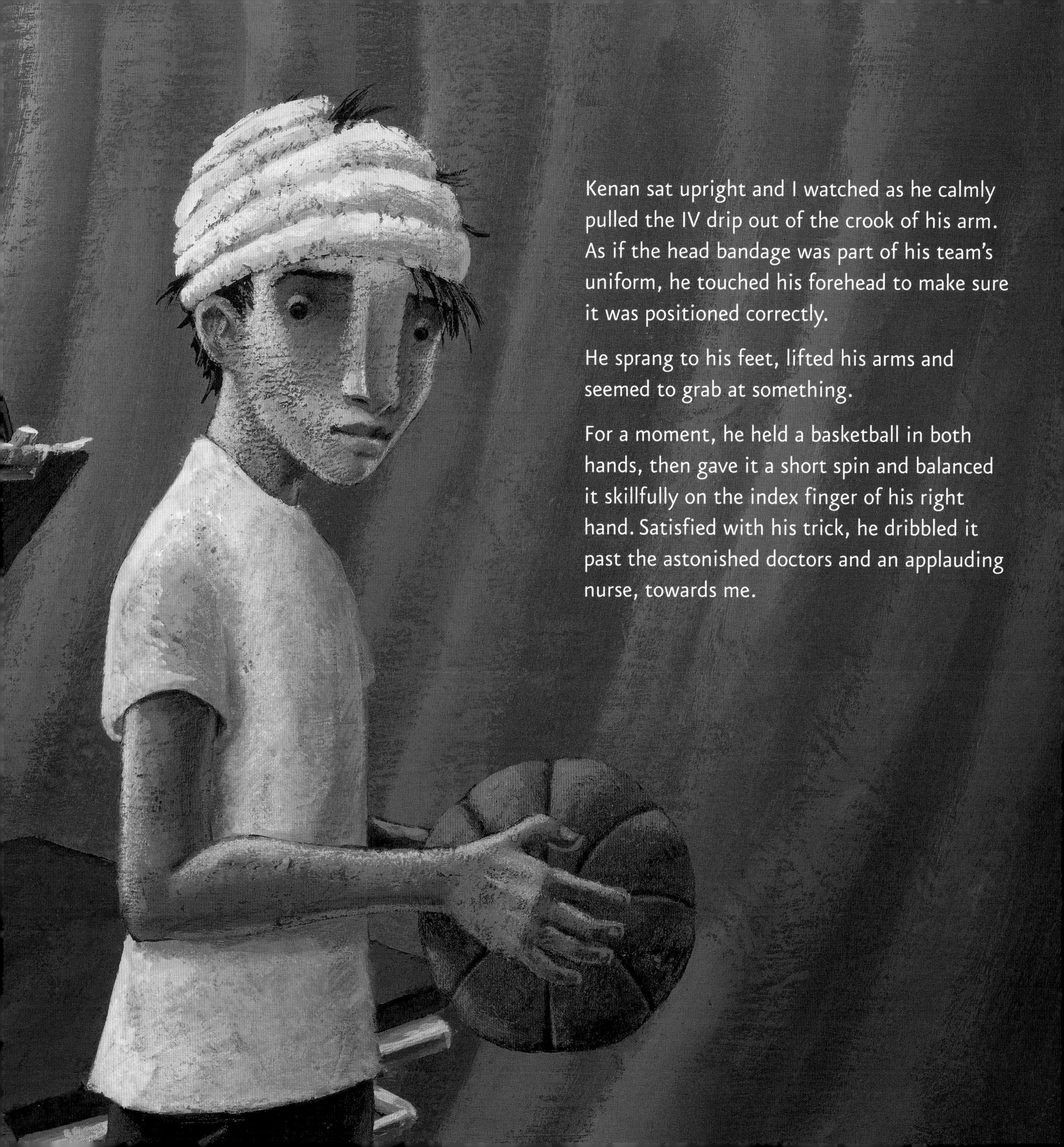

Kenan sat upright and I watched as he calmly pulled the IV drip out of the crook of his arm. As if the head bandage was part of his team's uniform, he touched his forehead to make sure it was positioned correctly.

He sprang to his feet, lifted his arms and seemed to grab at something.

For a moment, he held a basketball in both hands, then gave it a short spin and balanced it skillfully on the index finger of his right hand. Satisfied with his trick, he dribbled it past the astonished doctors and an applauding nurse, towards me.

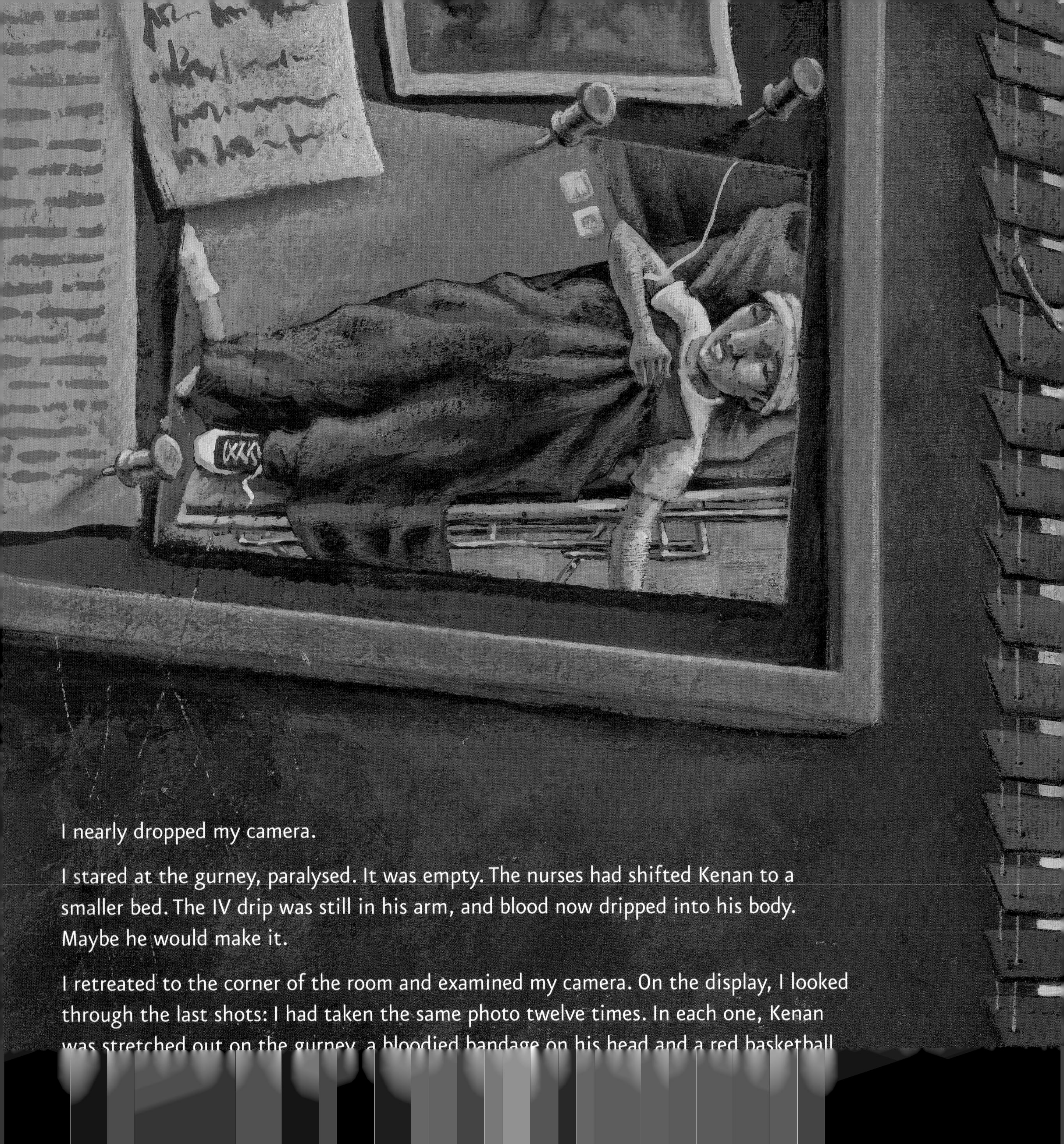

I nearly dropped my camera.

I stared at the gurney, paralysed. It was empty. The nurses had shifted Kenan to a smaller bed. The IV drip was still in his arm, and blood now dripped into his body. Maybe he would make it.

I retreated to the corner of the room and examined my camera. On the display, I looked through the last shots: I had taken the same photo twelve times. In each one, Kenan was stretched out on the gurney, a bloodied bandage on his head and a red basketball

"Hey champ! How's the basketball season going?"

On the other end of the line, my nephew sounded excited. "We have a real chance at the championship! If you're back in time, you have to come to the final game!"

"It would be a privilege! I'd love to be there! Take care of yourself until then!" And of your shoes, I wanted to tell him, but we had already hung up.

The World News
SCHOOLBUS
ATTACKED